whose mouse are you?

BY ROBERT KRAUS • PICTURES BY JOSE ARUEGO

MACMILLAN PUBLISHING COMPANY
New York

COLLIER MACMILLAN PUBLISHERS
London

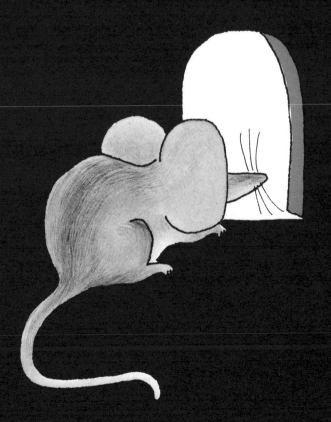

Macmillan Publishing Company
866 Third Avenue, New York, NY 10022

Collier Macmillan Canada, Inc.
ISBN 0-02-751190-1
Library of Congress Catalog Card Number: 70-89931

20   19   18   17

For Bruce and Billy

Whose mouse are you?

Nobody's mouse.

Where is your mother?

Inside the cat.

Where is your father?

Caught in a trap.

Where is your sister?

Far from home.

Where is your brother?

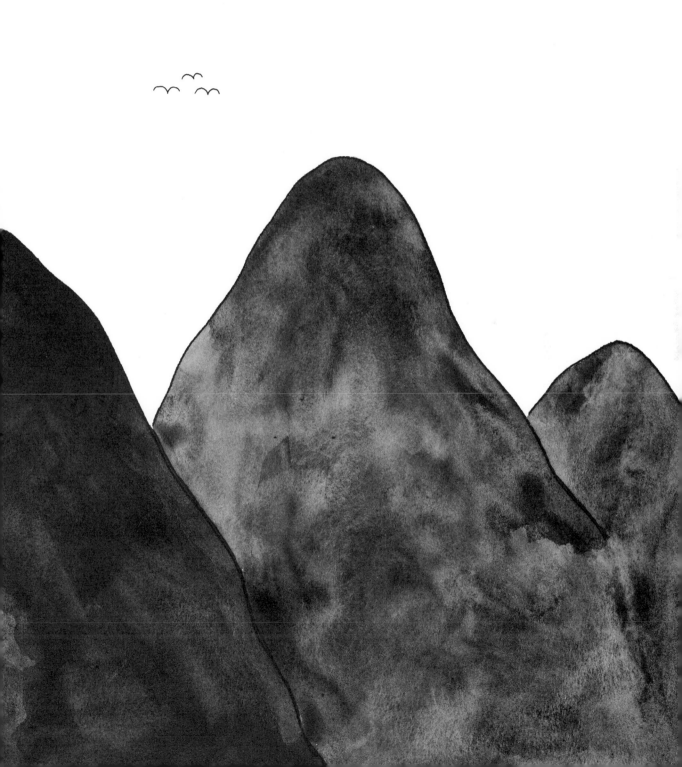

I have none.

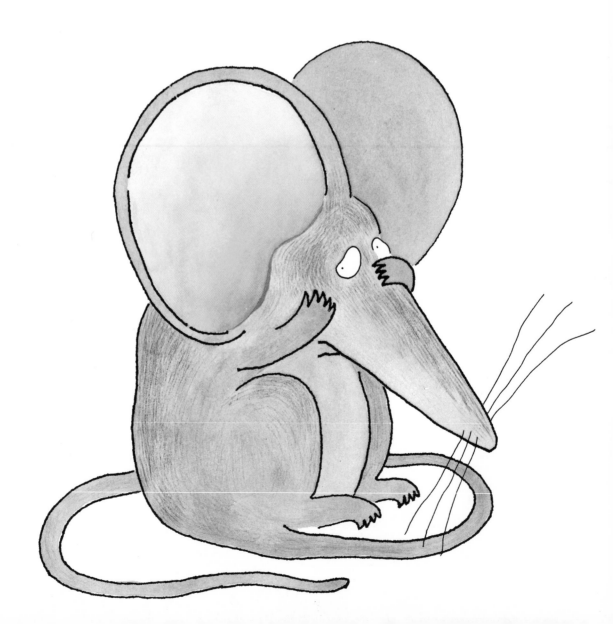

What will you do?

Shake my mother out of the cat!

Free my father from the trap!

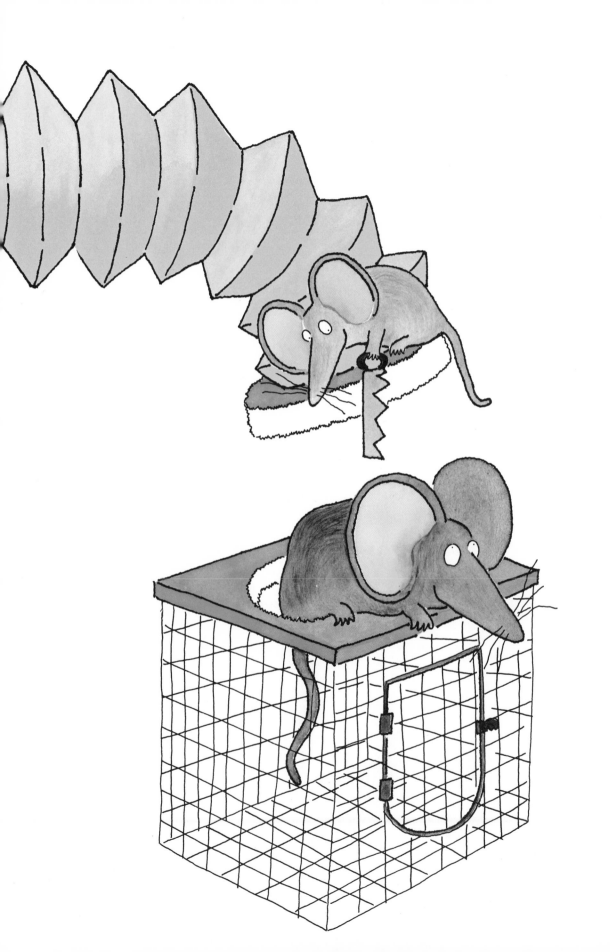

Find my sister and bring her home.

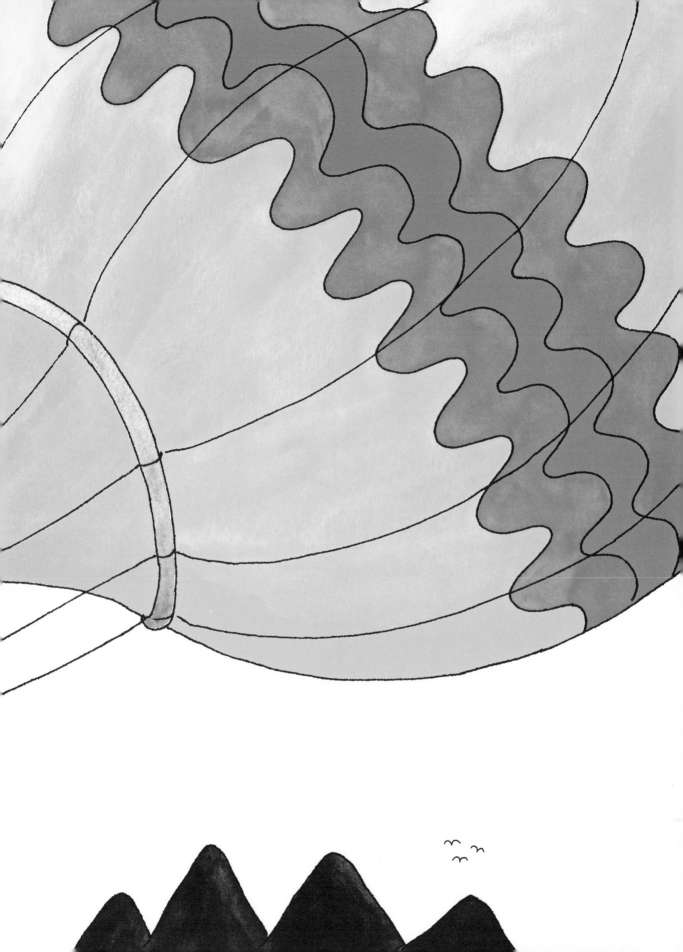

Wish for a brother as I have none.

Now whose mouse are you?

My mother's mouse, she loves me so.

My father's mouse, from head to toe.

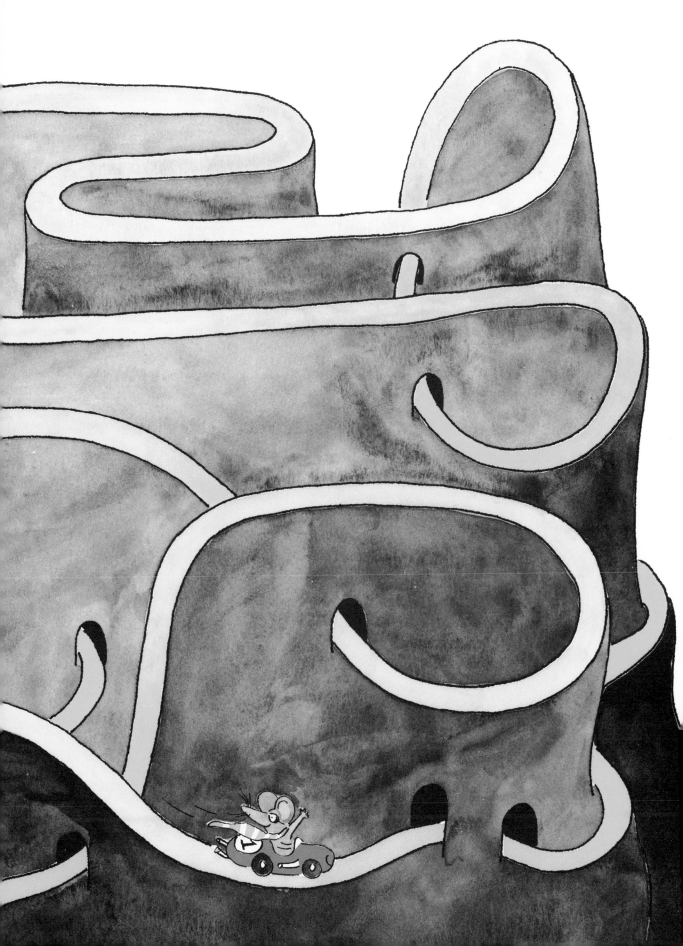

My sister's mouse, she loves me too.

My brother's mouse....

Your brother's mouse?

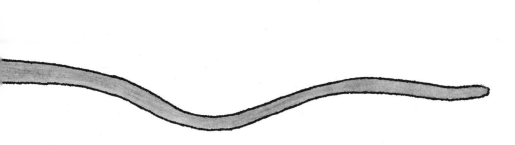

My brother's mouse—he's *brand* new!

Mauri